When You
to Us Bring Music

A guide to the psychological, spiritual and intellectual renewal of capitalism.

Michael Sclater

Contents

Preface

In an attempt to hold on to my sanity after being involved in the corporate world, I wrote an early version of this book more than 25 years ago.

Chief executives were struggling to satisfy their shareholders. Managers were struggling to meet their targets. Workers were doing what they were told. The result was that capitalism, which had improved the lives of so many, was now doing a great deal of harm - to people, cultures, health, wildlife, the soil, the environment, the climate and the planet. What was needed, in my view, was nothing less than profound change in the psychological, spiritual and intellectual foundations of capitalism.

At the time, my respectable friends thought I was nuts. But recently some of the surviving ones have said: 'You know that book you wrote years ago. I think you should do something with it. It matters'. It does. It matters so desperately that unless all of us make the kind of journey described here we may totally ruin ourselves and the planet. So here it is.

Today, we desperately don't want businesses to keep making money from a long list of products we regard as actively harmful - junk food, pesticides, awful farming and fishing techniques, cars running on fossil fuels, financial scams, unnecessary drugs, public services that don't work, unnecessary plastics, hideous housing …..the list goes on and on. We know that something profound in the whole operating system has to change.

Written in the form of a story set in the near future, here is how we can recreate capitalism so it meets our real longings. If you are in business it can show you a profitable and enjoyable way forward. Whoever you are, so long as we do it, here are some possible grounds for hope.

Chapter 1

THE ILLUSION OF SUCCESS

I was the attendant in an underground car park in the City of London. My name, by the way, is Djalal.

Each morning, I used to drive Sir Jeremy Jameson's Ferrari round the hairpin into its parking bay. On Fridays in the winter he usually came in his Range Rover if he was going shooting next day. In that case his two retrievers would be in the back and I would take them for a walk in the square at lunch time.

Sir Jeremy was chairman and chief executive of a business which people said made enormous amounts of money. One day I asked him about it. He said:

'Do you know what an investment company is?'

I said I thought it was to do with providing money for businesses. He laughed:

'We've moved beyond that. These days it's just about us making money. We can make money by buying businesses, selling businesses and betting whether shares will go up or down. We can bet that businesses will fail and even make them fail. We can take them over, load them with debt and then sell them for more than we paid. We can 'invest' in ruining the currency of entire nations and make fortunes from it. We can trade in so called financial products that are so complicated that almost no one understands them - at least until they realise how much money they have lost. We can programme computers to trade in shares so fast that we can make quick money. Do you have a mortgage Djalal?'

'I don't have a mortgage. I rent.'

'Ah. Well if you did have a mortgage we could make money out of trading that. Trading in ground rents is profitable too.'

As the lift came he said:

'It's capitalism Djalal. It's the game we play - and my job is to make sure we win.'

I first realised that Sir Jeremy was entering a period of crisis in the autumn of that year. His colleagues thought he was ill or stressed or even on the edge of having a breakdown. In a sense they were correct. But this was the kind of breaking down that occurs when a person's spirit struggles to emerge more fully. It is always painful – and it can end equally in triumph or disaster.

He took to leaving earlier in the evenings. From the mileage, I could see that he often went back to his flat instead of to his beautiful wife and estate in the country. His energy was fading. One Friday he said he did not want to go shooting, which he always did in the winter, but supposed he'd better go. I heard he was letting his colleagues do more, which was not like him at all. He gave up being managing director as well as chairman.

He took to chatting to me a little in the evenings. Once he said: 'I don't know, Djalal, what I'm doing all this for'. Then he would leave abruptly as if for something more important. I began to feel, not force and determination, but confusion. Some days, he did not come in at all.

One evening, he told me a strange story. Sometime before, two people from Germany had asked him to lunch. One was an aristocrat, he thought, and the other appeared to be his business manager. They said they had just sold an engineering business. They wanted Sir Jeremy's company to invest 380 million pounds for them. Before Jamesons could do this, they had to be careful that the origins of the money were legal. It must not come from drugs, for example. So they made checks. It was alright. So they did the deal. But later strange things happened. The two Germans asked Jamesons to open bank accounts for them. This was fairly normal. But then Jamesons were asked to make peculiar payments from these accounts. Often they were small sums like £60,000 to odd accounts in strange parts of the world. Sometimes large sums of money were received and Jamesons had to pay them immediately out again according to very exact timings. Sir Jeremy was worried. But nothing more would have happened were it not for a strange coincidence. One weekend an employee of Jamesons who was a keen sailor saw a yacht advertised which interested her. She found out it was being auctioned after being arrested with explosives and weapons on board. The owners had never come forward. But it was registered to an obscure company in Bermuda. The employee thought she recognised the name. It turned out to be one of those Jamesons had transferred money to. She told Sir Jeremy.

Sir Jeremy did not have to act. No one else had been told. He consulted his lawyer, quietly over lunch so no notes were taken. She said he had no need to lose a highly profitable client. But he was unsure. His lawyer was angry. In the end she said: 'Look, Jeremy, you have to decide whether you are in business in the City or not. You have no legal obligation to scan the yachting magazines in case one of your clients turns out to be not very nice.

So get on with it. Manage his money, which is what you are paid for.' Sir Jeremy said: 'He doesn't want it managed. He wants it laundered. And God knows what he does with it.'

Before he had always been certain. Now he was uncertain. He asked what I thought. I said I did not know. Of course I did know. So did he. But the universe was inviting Sir Jeremy to find out that he knew. It was not for me, Djalal, to do this work for him. Sir Jeremy glared at me, as if I was quite useless as he should have expected.

Some weeks later, his secretary Jean told me there was a terrible row in the office because Sir Jeremy had just sacked a profitable client without consulting anyone and giving no reasons. I was very pleased for him.

One morning, Sir Jeremy just sat in his car. I went to the door to see if he was alright. He said: 'I don't know that I can face this anymore, Djalal.' For a moment he was naked, searching like a child. I let him see a little of my heart, of my love. I saw the incomprehension in his eyes. I smiled. He pulled himself together. I thought of him beginning a journey from which there is never any return. A journey of the soul. I thought of the pain that was to come, and wished him well. I felt an urge to be helpful but then I thought: 'No Djalal, it is his journey. So mind your own business!' As I parked the Ferrari I said to it (I know it is silly to talk to a car, but I do): 'I think you may soon be parted from the dear person that owns you. But if he returns, he will be a much greater one.'

One Monday morning, about three months later, Sir Jeremy did not turn up at the office. I do not know how it happened or where he went. In the evening his secretary Jean showed me, with tears running down her cheeks, a note she had received. In Sir Jeremy's usual short way, it said:

Jean

I have decided to go away indefinitely. The business can manage without me.

Since there will be little for you to do here, I have arranged for you to see Sir Jack Hamilton in his office on Monday next at 7:30 a.m. He is, I understand, dissatisfied with his present arrangements.

Thank you for all you have done. Should you require further help, contact my solicitor who will be able to reach me.

With best wishes

Jeremy Jameson.

Years later Harold, his game keeper, showed me a similar note in which Sir Jeremy asked him to look after his dogs. His wife continued to live in the house in the country. Everyone was sympathetic to her over his appalling behaviour. In fact they had each become so isolated in their own suffering that Sir Jeremy's absence did not make all that much difference. Now, at least, she had even more time to do things of her own.

Chapter 2

BREAKDOWN

Sir Jeremy was away for more than six years. His friends, family and business colleagues heard almost nothing from him. Only his solicitor knew where he was. One week there was great excitement because the company had bet a lot of its money, and its clients' money, on the expectation that shares in American and British banks would collapse. When they did, which was not a great surprise because Jamesons had got hold of some useful information in advance, the company made not millions but billions. They became heroes. Even then, no one heard a word from Sir Jeremy.

I think I was the only one of his old contacts to see him. It was one night in the car park, about 2.00 am. He had been away nearly 3 years. Only one or two cars still had not gone home. Footsteps came slowly down the entrance ramp. I saw Sir Jeremy. He looked ill and exhausted. He was brown so he must have been in a hot country. I found out later he was in South America.

He said: 'Djalal, I came back to England for a few days ostensibly because I had to sign some papers. But I think it was partly because I wanted to see you. For some reason I have been incredibly angry with you. I have a crazy sense that you are in some way responsible for what has been happening to me. I've lost my job. I've cut myself off from my friends. I've been extremely ill. I'm in a state of complete confusion about everything. Most of the time I experience nothing but despair and hopelessness. I have found someone to help me, but like you she seems to be guiding me to get steadily worse. I feel that you and she are conspirators in taking me on some bewildering journey. I don't know what it is, or where it is going. But I can't give it up. There seems no way back to the normal life I once knew.

On top of that wild emotions pour through me like a hurricane over which I have no control. They are wearing me out. I was going to come here and confront you. I wanted to find out if you have been casting horrible Turkish spells on me. Or have I imagined all this?'

I did not answer. I just rested quietly, in love. Then he went on: 'But on the way here, everything changed. I began to take an obsessive interest in the manhole covers I was walking over. Have you ever noticed that many of them are extraordinarily beautiful? I realised that they have been made with ridiculous amounts of love. I felt completely connected to the anonymous craftsmen who made them. I was sharing with them some awesome, incredible joy. And then on a street corner I bumped into what I took to be a burglar and I saw into him. I saw right into his soul, Djalal. He looked at me with terror as if he had seen his maker. And then a bit later I went into a cafe and the old lady there for no apparent reason put her arms round me and then got terribly embarrassed. I have no idea what is going on. I suppose I am dying. It feels like it anyway.' I led him into my little office. I held him with my eyes.

When he was quieter, I said to him: 'You are not dying. But you are seeing things differently'. He nodded. I said: 'It is very frightening if it comes so strongly. But today, Sir Jeremy, we are colleagues. You see, the universe is not quite like people think it is. You know that now.' He went on looking at me, so seriously that I thought I had better say a little more: 'People have known experiences of this kind through all of history. It is what lies at the heart of all religions. It will change things for you. You are feeling more a part of this whole world, are you not, not just your little single self?' He nodded again, so I went on: 'In time you will want to serve the world more. It won't make things easier for you. In fact it may present all kinds of challenges. But it also brings tremendous joy. You are very fortunate.'

He sat quietly, for a long time. I made some tea. He looked at his tea and said: 'There are no drugs in this are there? Anything that's going to make me go even madder?' I said no. It was just tea. After a bit he said: 'Djalal, I have never really believed there is a God. I went to church and pretended to. I even read the lesson. Is there one?'

I said 'No'. He looked disappointed, as if I had taken away his last shred of hope. I wasn't going to feed fairy stories to him. I went on: 'But neither is there not a God. I have a feeling that God does not exactly exist or not exist. He's beyond all that.'

Sir Jeremy said: 'That's not much help to me'. I said: 'On the contrary. You have just realised that things can exist and not exist, be here and there, have you not?' I saw his eyes fixed on me. I felt his heart come up into his throat so the emotion prevented him from speaking. Mine followed. The whole universe was flowing between us.

When he was ready I went on: 'What we do know – and you have just found out – is that deep, deep inside us is a sense of joy. It only comes when our usual thoughts and feelings and opinions about everything get out of the way. And when it comes, those other things that are talked about in all the world's religions come with it; like love and compassion. So do other qualities which today's seekers often lose sight of, like strength and fearlessness. You have always had these qualities. So you see, you have always been a man of spirit.'

He waited a long time again in silence. Then he said: 'So is there only just me? No one else to lean on?' I said: 'In a way that is true. The more we discover ourselves, the more we realise our utter, terrible aloneness. There is, as you say, no one else to lean on. But then a strange thing happens. You find that this joy of yours is somehow the same as everyone else's. And everything else's. This is what we can call God if we wish. It is what makes everything happen. It is what everything is. Is that enough for you?' After a long pause, Sir Jeremy said: 'I believe it is. Or it could be, one day.'

After more silence, Sir Jeremy said: 'I am starting to see why I feel such enormous fear. I am being taken over by some kind of energy over which I have no control. In other words, my sense of 'I' is under severe threat. That's tough after 50 years of rather successful efforts to build it up.'

I said: 'I know. Leaving behind your Eton and Oxford is hard is it not? It is by the way just as hard to leave behind being a business person from Turkey who was also rather respected for his learning. But you must not think that afterwards nothing is left. On the contrary. Underneath it all is a real Sir Jeremy who you are now discovering. This real Sir Jeremy is unique. And so you will have your own unique way of expressing this energy that you talk about. It is all one, but we express it in our own ways. For some of us, even in car parks!' We laughed together.

Finally, he looked at me with a kind of wonder and said: 'Djalal, why am I talking to you about all this?' I said: 'Because I am, more or less, just me. You have not met many people like that. So it fascinates you.' I wasn't going to tell him that I knew all the great spiritual works. Nor that I had practised under the guidance of my master for many years. Then he would have set off on a journey with his head. This was the last thing we needed. I knew his friend in South America understood this too.

I was tired and wanted to go home. I asked if he had somewhere to go. He said he had. We embraced. I told him not to expect this state to last and he looked very disappointed. He left by taxi. Some things don't change. I never told anyone of this before.

Chapter 3

SIR JEREMY RETURNS

Three more years passed.

One evening in April, I saw a headline in a paper. It said 'Return of Missing Investment Genius'. It was about Sir Jeremy. A reporter had recognised him at the airport. She had followed him to his home in the country. Much to everyone's surprise, he was with Lady Jameson there. Next week, there was a picture of the two of them together. They were going for a walk, holding hands, like lovers.

A few weeks later, everyone in the company and a few others (such as me) received an invitation to spend a weekend with the Jamesons. It was more of an instruction than an invitation, I think. It was nice for an old immigrant like me to be included. We were to get on a boat at Westminster pier the next Friday at 2.00 pm. It would take us up the Thames to the Jamesons' house in the country.

I remember I surprised everyone by wearing my traditional clothes. Late in the evening, after passing through many locks, we arrived at the jetty on Sir Jeremy's estate. He was waiting.

When he left the company, his body had been heavy and thick. Now, he was lithe and stood easily. His energy seemed to contain within it some kind of magnetism, and I noticed how people liked to stand near him. He welcomed everyone quietly. His voice, which used to pretend, was now deep and beautiful.

We met with joy. We both cried a little. Both of us had known much loneliness. It was good to have company.

That night, we all chatted for a bit around a fire. Sir Jeremy was unassuming. He carried drinks about and made sure everyone was alright. I felt the atmosphere begin to soften.

I heard some young dealers taking bets on what Sir Jeremy had got them together for. They thought he might apologise for being away, or thank them for all they had done, or maybe announce his retirement. Perhaps he had sold the business and they might lose their jobs. Possibly he simply wanted to meet them all. I didn't know either. But I knew they were all wrong.

Sir Jeremy had booked everyone except me into an expensive hotel for the night. I was in his house.

In the morning, we gathered – about 150 of us – in one of the barns, in a circle. Most sat on chairs. The younger sat on cushions on the floor. This is what Sir Jeremy said, on that Saturday morning. I have copied it out from a tape that someone made.

By way of introduction, he said: 'Welcome'. That was all. Ah, I thought, you have indeed travelled, Sir Jeremy. He did not say sorry for his disappearance or his long absence. He was not at all sorry. So he did not say so. He said simply what he felt, just then.

'I want to discuss with you some ideas I have for the company.

They have all grown out of my experiences while I have been away, so I will tell you about them in that context.

After I left, I finished up in Chile. I rented a run-down small holding with a cottage on it. It was high in some hills, with no services of any kind and no neighbours for miles. I thought that, by just being quiet for a while, I might rediscover some sense in my life.

Well, what happened was I had more time to get even

more miserable and confused! There were no appointments to let me escape from myself. Not even a telephone. I began to realise that, if I was ever to get out of the misery I was in, I had to have some help.

One day I drove, in an old truck I had bought, to the local town to shop. I remember shopping at the grocer's stall in the market pretending, very successfully I thought, to be alright. Beside me an oldish lady started to bumble about looking for nice things. I was a bit offended when the people in the stall paid much more attention to her than they did to me. Then she looked at me in that way that Djalal has that seems to very gently lay everything bare. She made some polite remarks in English with what seemed a slightly South American accent. Then she said: 'If you would like to come and see me, they can tell you here where I am. You would be most welcome.' Then she left.

Some months later, when I was desperate enough, I called again at the shop. They knew little about her. Only, they spoke as if it was obvious to everyone that she was someone special. Apparently she lived on a small farm with her husband about 40 miles away. Feeling at the same time excited and extremely foolish, I drove to see her. When I arrived she smiled as if my arrival was the most natural thing in the world and invited me in.

I saw her once or twice a week for 4 years. I have never

loved anyone so deeply, nor been so astonished by anyone's insight and knowledge. I believe she was part therapist and part teacher. She taught from her own experience, but I believe it was the same as has always been taught by such people within all the world's great spiritual traditions. Here name was Vara.

So what did I learn that might be relevant to this business?

One thing I realised was that I was exhausted. I don't just mean that I was tired and needed a rest. It felt as if my work and indeed whole life had been drawing on a finite bank of vitality and slowly running it down. There was now precious little left.

As I got to know myself more, I began to understand the reason. All my life I had been acting a part from a script written by others – family, school masters, friends and society. I had followed their goals, morality, manners and ways of doing things. There was nothing necessarily wrong with this script. The problem was that what I was doing, and the way I was, was not coming from the inner core that I was very slowly beginning to discover inside me. Therefore, I had been continually fighting against myself. No wonder I was worn out!

If I am to come back into business life, I know that I have to do so in a way that feels in tune with the person I really am. I do believe there is such a person, who I get closer to as I gradually strip away the layers of convention and habits and prejudices that obscure him. If I don't I'll disintegrate. If I do, the energy will flow out from the centre and I'll be alive. It is part of my dream, too, that all of you might have a better chance of doing the same.

Another reason for my exhaustion was that I had been unconsciously struggling to repress layer upon layer upon layer of fear. I was frightened of being genuinely open with anyone else, as opposed to talking to them politely. I was frightened of being an ordinary person instead of someone special. I was frightened of any little gap in my diary because then I might be faced with the unbearable question: 'Who, really, am I, Jeremy Jameson?' I had a lot of fear about mundane things too, like not having enough money in my old age or losing my health. In the end all these fears rather resolved themselves into one big fear. Actually an enormous fear. The fear of dying.

I realised that being the great Sir Jeremy Jameson in the City was in large measure a way of trying to bury all these fears. By bringing as much as possible under my power and control, how could there be anything to fear? The snag was, the fear kept growing.

Well, over the last few years I've lived with those fears and – slowly and painfully – they've receded. I'm more able these days to be just me. So I'm no longer interested in the business as a rather deceitful support system. I see it instead as a vehicle to enable me, and hopefully all of you too, to do things that feel really good and worthwhile to us. Quite a change!'

As Sir Jeremy spoke, I felt my heart open more and more. Besides his words, Sir Jeremy was radiating a kind of light. The others were affected too even though they could not yet see, with their heads, how Jameson & Co could ever be different. He went on:

'As my journey continued, I also discovered in myself an immense amount of buried anger. It came surging up so it would take me over for days and weeks on end. Some of this anger was about things that had happened in my childhood. It was due to anything that people had done, usually entirely unknowingly, that had scarred my soul in some way. Eventually, I discovered in myself a kind of primitive rage that dated from my first few weeks of life, due to my opinion at the time that I was not getting as much love, or milk, or cuddles, as I felt I had a right to expect.

I realise now that, in my working life, I had often been unconsciously expressing this deep anger. It drove me on to burn out employees, take companies over, downsize, asset strip and drive faster than others on the roads. It drove me to push myself ever harder and harder. Of course it was invariably justified by respectable business jargon, like efficiency and competitiveness.

As this anger surfaced into consciousness, it dissipated. Don't ask me how. It just did. So in future I'd like to work without being driven by all that anger. I want to work with more gentleness towards myself, others and the environment. And when there is anger, I don't want to act it out by harming others.

Another uncomfortable thing that I slowly became aware of was my tendency to violence. In my case it would come up mainly in my emotional attitude to anyone I thought not as right as me. I could see how this emotional violence can very easily escalate - as we can see every day in the news - into physical violence. I refuse to blame myself for this. This aspect of us has evolved, alongside our capacity for love, as sometimes necessary for survival. I won't even blame myself for the thrill that often comes with it. But I do desperately regret the times when a covert thrill of violence has governed my actions in business. For example, when we invested in a development that we knew would destroy another habitat, a waste management company with environmental credentials that we all knew were fake or a care business that we knew would succeed by more effective exploitation of the staff. On a global scale, we are currently viciously destroying what is surely dearest to most of us – our own planet.

In future, I want to admit to this strange darkness in myself, but I do not want to express it. I want to express the light.

This applies equally, by the way, to our own working conditions. At present, do we really need to work so hard or is there also an element of actually wishing to destroy ourselves? Why does a rich company like us have almost no natural light, hopeless ventilation and windows that don't open? Why do we zap ourselves with an electronic smog from computers and photocopiers? Why do we eat food that is lifeless and contaminated? Why do we wear drab and uncomfortable suits? Why is the office so stark, as if to stamp out our humanity? Let's see if we can treat ourselves better.

I found that I was deeply attached to a primitive notion of what it is to be a man. I thought the idea was to be tough and thrusting and to get my way by triumphing at all costs over all that stood in my way. Well, these qualities can have their place. But then I found that the whole realm of what are usually referred to as 'feminine' qualities was present in me too. And it's often more effective and congenial to be, for example, soft, patient and accommodating.'

Sensing that some of those listening understood that he

had become weak, he said: 'Be careful though, because the man or woman in whom these opposites meet is a force to be reckoned with!

Something else that I don't want to go far into now – because we would be here for a week – is my discovery of how attached I was to a whole raft of ideas that underpinned my work. I'd sometimes come up with my usual stock opinions on subjects like politics, business and society to Vara and she would just look at me. Everyone else I'd ever met would collude with the same ideas, so we'd have a nice comfortable conversation. But she wouldn't. And then I'd think: 'Oh God, Jeremy, you've never even begun to think that one through. You've taken on board a lot of nonsense that just happens to be the flavour of the times. You could take a dozen different views, and see it from a dozen different directions, and they might all be equally right.'

I'll mention just one of these naive assumptions of mine. It's the one that says that competitiveness lies at the heart of the success of all modern business. So we all compete furiously, between each other, between companies and between nations. Competitiveness is now the unchallenged rallying call of all governments.

Well, when I think about it, do I want competitiveness to be a guiding principle in my life? Do I want to compete with colleagues or would it be nicer to work with them?

Do I want to put friends who work in a company in a similar area to mine out of business? Do I want Britain to do better than those nice people where I go on holiday? Do I want to compete with nature – which nowadays is always the loser? Do I want to compete with others on the roads? Do I want to compete with the homeless in the streets? Well......No! I want the best for all of them.

And is competitiveness really a factor in success? Certainly it can help to push us towards excellence. But in the longer run I believe cooperation is the real key to success. We can see this in the animal world as well as in our own. It's a myth that animals survive (as natural scientists used to say they did) by winning in a ruthless struggle for survival. When we observe them, we see that they build homes, care for their young, play, sunbathe, interact socially and as far as we can see care for one another. These are the real keys to their success.

Lastly, I'd like to mention something else that came up again and again throughout my adventure. This was the most profound grief. It seemed to follow whenever the fear and anger subsided.

At first this grief was mostly personal, around the hurts I had suffered and inflicted and all the time I had wasted in so much ignorance. In time though it extended to more universal things beyond my own immediate involvement, to things like the murder of the Native Americans, the cutting down of rain forests, the misuse of drugs by the medical profession, and the spreading of misinformation on a global scale by public relations companies.

I despaired and grieved especially at the awesome emotional immaturity that drives the Western world. I understood, more and more profoundly, why a tribe in South America that has managed to retain some of its old culture refers to the White man as 'Little Brother'.

Because of this grief, for a long time I found it too painful to think of rejoining mainstream activity, with all its cruelty, competitiveness and destruction. Many, I think who follow this same adventure get stuck here. They drop out or join protest groups from which to snap angrily from the sidelines.'

I remember Sir Jeremy paused for a long time here. Many in the room were looking inwards and knowing that what he said was true. In the end one of the young clever people who Sir Jeremy had not yet met asked a question. His name was Roger. He said:

'But Sir Jeremy, we ordinary people have to keep going don't we? The world isn't going to stop just because it's not as nice as you'd like it to be. You've made your fortune. I'm still working on next term's school fees. I don't have these choices that you talk about.'

Sir Jeremy said: 'I hear what you say. But I think you have

more choices than you realise. You could leave the business couldn't you? You could find another job. Your child might do fine at a local school, or studying at home. So you do have choices.' I saw anger flare in the young man. He was being invited to go outside his usual pattern of thinking. He didn't like it!

Sir Jeremy went on: 'I do agree with you, however, that it would be much more enjoyable to keep the business going. To go back to my story, at the time I could not see any way of doing so, or any reason for doing so.

The key to this came in an unexpected way. After so much suffering, I found almost despite myself that a deep sense of joy was gradually growing. It would break out in me, sometimes for hours, then days and then even weeks.

With this joy came a knowledge that somehow everything is alright. A knowledge too that things are not as separate as they seem; in fact they are somehow the same. This is the beginning of love. It is not a selective love. It is not a love for good people who do good things but not for bad people who do bad things; not for beauty but not ugliness, gentleness but not harshness, honesty but not dishonesty, health but not illness, some political systems but not others and so on. It is an increasing acceptance of everything. Things are as they are.

It was in getting glimpses of this that I found myself

wishing to rejoin the commercial fray. It's alright after all. To stand outside the commercial world would be to reject it, and that I do not do. I would be expressing not my connectedness with creation but my disconnectedness, separation. I was about to come back and give the world the benefit of my services.

What I hadn't realised was that the hardest part of the journey was yet to come. I would prefer not to take time telling you about it but I feel it may help you. If you make a similar journey – and I expect many of you are already – you'll find that in one way or another it is a stage that has to be faced. It is the stage of the pupil leaving his or her teacher.

It happened for me, unexpectedly, just as I was preparing to return to England. Some thieves broke into Vara's home. By ill luck, she and a friend returned to the house and came upon them. They were outlaws who had no other means of survival. Vara told them they could take all they liked and sat down calmly. But, according to the friend, they reacted to her calmness by becoming increasingly disturbed. Her quiet presence revealed their own incredible pain to them in a way that was unbearable. As they left she stood and opened her hands slightly as if in a gesture of acceptance. They tried the only way to escape that they could manage. They turned and shot her. Her friend, who was terrified and hysterical, they ignored. They left with the equivalent of about £70 in English money.

I experienced a more agonising grief than I had ever conceived as being possible. But there was more than that. I realised that much of what I thought I knew was actually what she knew. The love that I felt was actually her enormous love; I had not really owned it for myself.

I fell back into despair. There I was in the middle of nowhere, with no teacher, no prospects and not even any longer the excitement of my personal and spiritual journey to keep me going. I was in a desert; utterly barren and seemingly without end.

Eventually, it dawned on me that something was happening even more profound than the mystical experience of being flooded with love or joy or a sense of unity. I was beginning to accept myself. At last I found that I could potter about in my field, or sit on the veranda with a cup of tea, and be content. This was when I knew I was really ready at last to come back.'

These words from the chairman took up the morning. There was silence. Everyone had stopped pretending. I saw tears in the eyes of some of the toughest and most feared city predators. In a corner of the barn a mouse rootled about. 'My goodness, little mouse,' I thought, 'these people are beginning to grow up.' I heard the birds singing outside. I knew that, even if nothing more happened outwardly, Sir Jeremy had changed the company for ever. He had given them permission to be open and truthful. They could never go back on that. But I wondered what would happen once they all had some time to think.

I did not have long to wait. At lunch, some looked condescendingly at Sir Jeremy as they might at a poor lunatic who had just come out of mental hospital; in time, with luck and tolerance, he might get over it and become a normal person like them again! Others were embarrassed and laughed and giggled. A cuddly looking man with a pipe, which he caressed like his dearest friend, had such strong defences that he carried on as usual, pretending that Sir Jeremy had not said anything remarkable. Many, I think, were very frightened. A few looked excited. They were too excited, I thought, as if they had found some wonderful new father to lead them forwards and make them feel good. I was happy when I heard one of the older people say quietly to another: 'I feel things could change. But the question of how is so enormous I can hardly grasp it. And who are we to do it? Any why should it be us?' Here was someone who would, I knew, be useful.

As I wandered about I heard someone say: 'Is this all the fault of a car park attendant? I knew the immigration rules need tightening'. I smiled – but it hurt as well. When I had coffee I met a weather beaten person who was Sir Jeremy's game keeper. I thought he might be a monster. But he was completely alive. I knew he had recognised and understood every word.

After lunch, the sun was out. I went to the river. Sir Jeremy was there, by himself. Our eyes met, with pleasure. There was nothing to say. I left him to his little space of quiet.

Chapter 4

CAPITALISM IN QUESTION

After the break the Chairman went on:

'So, for me the question now is: what am I going to do with myself?

Well, I would like if possible to continue with Jamesons.

But I can only do so if I can follow, as best I can, the sort of inner drives that I have been talking about. I refer to these collectively as my spirit. I have no doubt that you all share something similar although you may have a different name for it – your nature, your humanity, what you can't help caring about, the universe or even God.

I want us to give ourselves permission to incorporate this spirit more into our work. I want it understood that our spirit is not just part of our work. It *is* our work'.

Sir Jeremy paused for a long time to let this extraordinary thought take life in the room. In the end one of Roger's friends called out:

'If that's what people want they can join a monastery.'

Roger said: 'If I tell any of the people I talk to each day that I'm incorporating spirit into my work that will be the last deal I do. It's the jungle we work in, not some kind of corporate paradise.'

Sir Jeremy said: 'Roger, I really respect what you say. But my point is that, in the course of this century, we have somehow slid into a situation where possibly a majority of people go to work to do more or less the opposite of the things they really care about. We have to get out of it. The really horrifying thing is that it's so familiar that we hardly even notice it. Humanity has somehow made it respectable to declare war on itself.

We can't go on in this way. It's making people ill and causing the most tremendous pain. Work, instead of being one of our greatest pleasures, is now for many a source of stress. So let's try to reintegrate our work with the way we really are.

I'd like to consider a bit more closely what our work is actually for.' One of Sir Jeremy's oldest colleagues said:

'Realistically, Jeremy, it's because we need to make money.'

Sir Jeremy said: 'I don't think it's so simple. Lots of people who don't need to make money work like anything - like parents who stay at home, many pensioners and people who've long since made enough not to have to work anymore.'

Someone else said: 'Well then it's to produce things. Unless we get on with it the place will fall apart. There'll be no houses, cars, TV and all that.'

Sir Jeremy said: 'Of course that's part of it. But a fraction of the population could do it all. That's how it already is actually. The majority of workers are not producing anything that anyone particularly needs.

I think the need to work is really to do with our spirit. There is a fundamental urge in us to get up to something. Just as subatomic particles apparently cannot sit about in a state of inertia, nor can we. We have to express ourselves in some way. You can take many views as to what it is we wish to express. You might say it is your individual ego. I think it is bigger than that. What we ultimately have is this burning desire to express love. That is the true point of our work. Robbed of it, we atrophy and die.

All the more amazing, then, that we have built a culture

of work that in many ways specifically excludes love. I heard these words some time ago from one of our best known colleagues in the City on a TV program.

As a market operator I work within the rules of the market and am not concerned with the social consequences of my actions.

This could be the epitaph of Western civilisation!'

Everyone laughed. Roger and his friends looked furious.

'So let's think of our work in a different way. Its purpose is to express our love.

If the purpose of our work is to express love, what then is the purpose of our business? Well, it's the vehicle to enable us to express our love, our spirit.

Now the enormous question is – and this is where I agree with Roger – how on earth could we set about this? We can maybe manage the intention. But what more than that?

Obviously I have some ideas on this. But I have learned that ideas and plans have most value if they are really owned by the people involved. So I would like to hand over to you now, for you to explore and carry them forward – if you would like to.'

There was a long silence. No one responded. Those who had hoped he would lead them forward to some wonderful new future looked downcast. Then he went on:

'First, I hope you will stay as long as you can this evening and tomorrow to talk about this more. Not only with me and among yourselves but also with Djalal. He may seem a humble man to you, but that is because in many ways he knows much more than us. I am honoured and grateful, Djalal, to have you with us.'

'Good heavens' I thought, 'what does he want me to do? Read them the Upanishads? Teach them dervish dancing? Give discourses on non-attachment? No No. He just wants me to patiently allow them to be open and chat if they wish to.'

'Second', Sir Jeremy went on, 'let's, tomorrow, try and decide how we might carry these ideas forward.

Allow me one word of caution. Any change we make will mean moving into the unknown. There will be no familiar old rules or nice established ways of doing things. This will be terrifying. But if one quality characterises a person of real spirit from any other, it is daring to imagine a different way forward. So let's try to do that. None of us knows what is going to happen. But something could!

How would it be if we meet again at 8.00 tomorrow morning?'

Someone suggested 9.00 to give them more time to enjoy

the country and talk informally among themselves, and this was agreed.

Chapter 5

THE LIST OF INVISIBLE PRODUCTS

Roger and a few others left in the evening. I knew that in the morning they would be contacting the agencies that get those people jobs. Sir Jeremy wanted to argue with them but I stood beside him and he let them go easily. It was not for him to decide what they would do. The others stayed.

When Roger and the others had gone, we found they had done us all a favour. A sense of comradeship grew among us who were left. We were involved. A die had been cast, as you say.

In the morning we all met up at 9.00.

As they talked, I understood how clever they were. Given some new ideas, they needed very little time to take them up. But they were not yet imaginative. Only Sir Jeremy had broken out of the prison of old rules and ideas that most people live in – even though no one tells them to.

They decided to make a special team to explore how they could express their spirit more in their work. At first they thought that anyone who wanted could be on it. Then they thought this would be inefficient. They agreed on a team of six. A young manager called Leon volunteered to co-ordinate it. This was agreed. Leon was a big rugby player and not one of the cleverest people there. But he had an instinct for the way things were going. If ever anyone made a good career move he did. Then they chose the other five. Then a woman who had been chatting with me in the evening before said:

'I'd like to propose Djalal for the team.' I protested: 'But I know nothing at all about your business.' Leon said: 'I think that may be exactly why we need you'. I could think of nothing to say. So then we were 7! Someone cheered and everyone laughed.

The team was to meet once a week. The company's computer system would enable anyone in the business to feed in ideas.

After the weekend, Sir Jeremy was back at his desk. He

was there for three rather short days a week. They talked about his ideas a lot. Often, they hung about in the car park before leaving, talking, talking. Some of them liked to have a cup of tea with me in my tiny office. One evening several important members of the staff were crammed in there deciding whether to leave or not. They asked what I thought. I smiled and said I didn't think it mattered much. That did it. They stayed.

Young Roger, on the other hand, avoided me as if I was spreading some kind of disease. He was so angry! Soon he found himself another job and left. I expect it was him who talked to someone in the newspapers. There was a story that Sir Jeremy Jameson had come back with weird ideas and was going to change the company. A lot of investors rang up to say they were concerned. But Sir Jeremy had his old skills. He said he was naturally 'Considering all possibilities' and that the company was always 'Looking at any ideas for improving its services to its customers.' They were used to assurances like these and were happy.

At our first meeting Leon passed round sheets of paper with ideas on from different people in the business. We read them for a bit. In the end he said:

'Well, we've got ideas that include linking up with the local church, doing voluntary work, sponsoring yet another environmental project and starting a holistic business school. I counted 18 suggestions for a statement of corporate values. What do you think?' I was watching an extremely stylish looking lady, about 55, called Veronica. I thought she might be made of diamond. But I liked her as well. Instead of replying she gave a long loud yawn. In case someone had not understood, she belched. You English can be amazing! Leon said: 'I agree.'

They talked more. Then they were silent and a bit miserable.

Then a thin worried looking person with glasses said: 'I think the problem is we are nowhere near ready for such specific ideas yet. Anyway, we've heard all of them dozens of times before. Mostly from other people's PR departments. The only way I can think this could get interesting is if we could somehow conceive of this whole company in an entirely different way.'

'That would be nice' someone said. Veronica made her back even straighter to show she might be interested. The thin worried one went on: 'Jeremy is effectively inviting us to reinvent the entire intellectual structure that makes capitalist business work. This is where we have to start, or we're not going to get anywhere.'

It sounded true. They agreed that this was where to begin. I cannot remember all the conversations. My English was not so good then and I did not understand all their words. Also, you see, they think with their heads. I think more somehow with my head and my heart all at once; it's different. After about three meetings Leon sent a note to everyone with a summary. Here are some bits that I think were interesting.

'If the purpose of our business becomes to express our spirit, what happens to profit? Jeremy, in the past, has told us all dozens of times that the business has one point only – to make a profit. If we lose sight of this for one moment, he used to say, we lose focus and die. Profit is constrained only by the law, a chance of getting caught or possible adverse public relations effects.

Well, what shall we think now?

It occurs to us that the business world has fallen into an elementary error. This is to confuse objectives and strategy. Every fresh recruit straight out of business school is supposed to know that an objective is what you want to do. Strategy is how you get there. Profit, throughout the developed world, has become mistaken for an objective. It's not. It's a strategy. It's like saying that the objective of Rugby is to win points. Is this really why someone sets off for a game? Of course not. People play because it is something worthwhile that they want to do. They do though keep a tally of how well they are doing. That's good strategy because it helps keep your eye on the ball.

We think that elevation of profit into an objective has had an understandable attraction for emotionally and spiritually immature people in the West. It provides an opportunity to escape from the complexities of being human into a simplistic world with a single goal. Veronica compares the business world to an old dinosaur with an extremely simple brain. It can only manage one idea at a time. It can get hold of profit. But the infinitely complex interplay of feelings is way beyond it. So it invents a doctrine that simply leaves them out. When confronted by the uncomfortable existence of the poor, the starving, the lonely, wrecked environments and devastated cultures, it simply says it knows profit is the best thing for them so it must be doing the best it can.

If possible, we would like to become more sophisticated than the old dinosaur!

So we could make profit part of Jameson & Co's *strategy*. Its *objective* would be to express our spirit in some way.

But what would 'expressing our spirit' mean in practice? As a start, how would we know whether we are doing so or not?

As Jeremy said, we know if we listen to our intuition. Pritpal, our Indian expert, says that in Indian psychology there is an aspect of our minds called 'Buddhi' which has the ability to access a higher form of knowledge that can

42

guide us. All we have to do, he says, is tune in and listen. Unfortunately, however, we don't hear much of such a thing in the West. We need something more tangible.

One criterion is whether or not what we are doing is useful. Does it on the whole benefit others in some way, or the environment or the whole planet even? Does it in some way move us a little closer to the dreams we all have about what would make our world a nicer place to live in?

We need to look carefully at what is useful today. A lot of what we have got used to thinking of as useful no longer is.

Just gambling on the markets certainly seems pretty useless.

It is not necessarily useful for us to help others produce more and more goods. They eat up resources and energy. The factories make a mess. In the developed countries, it would be actively useful to produce *less* of many of today's goods: cigarettes, pesticides, fertilisers, oil, gas, roads, cars, junk food, drugs, pornography, violence on TV. Frighteningly, these are some of the staples of our economy.

It is often not useful for us to help companies to become ever bigger. It's boring being sold the same shampoo and the same burgers wherever we go in the world. Those local people probably could have provided something more interesting – and enjoyed doing so. So if we go further with these ideas we may not have a great future in the take-over market either.

Equally, it would not be useful for us to help companies simply because they are creative. Creativity has got out of hand. It leads to faster cars that cause more accidents, more sophisticated ways to catch the remaining fish in the sea, more contaminated food, more blood curdling videos, more highways to every unspoiled corner of the world and even - can you believe it - creating new viruses. A lot of what passes for creativity is in reality destructive.

We worried that it is not for us to decide what is useful for others or not. But we can get round this. The thing for us to do is to ask whether a product or activity is something that would nourish us personally, that we would find useful. Could we produce it with love? Would it be worthy of our attention and quality? If so it will nourish others. You can justify this on the grounds that Jeremy talked about, that we and others are not really as separate as we might think.

Our problem now is: If we're to follow these ideas, we effectively rule out a great deal of our existing business. We'd cut our activities in the spot market by about 90%. Profits from mergers, takeovers and demergers might fall by about 80%. Foreign exchange dealings likewise. Loans to hedge funds would fall to zero. Nearly all of our share dealings would be excluded. Terrific!

So the question is: somewhere in all of this, could there conceivably be some kind of corresponding opportunity?'

That was the end of Leon's note. They were stuck here for a long time. They came up with endless ideas for new projects. They kept getting lost in discussing ways to make the business nicer to work in, which were not about being useful. They felt they were looking in a wrong direction – but could not think of any other directions. They went back to thinking of different goods. They thought of new sorts of services. They discussed how the information and computer business might be more useful. All they had found, so far, was a way of making Jamesons very holy, poor and dull. Veronica said: 'I think we're planning our way to looking like an Oxfam shop.'

One afternoon Sir Jeremy came down to see me in the car park. He looked sad. He said that now he was back at work he found it hard to stay in touch with his quiet centre. That sense of joy was not so easy to find whenever he wanted it. He was beginning to feel in a hurry and stressed like before. Also, it was hard to allow his dream to develop without controlling it. In the past he would have consulted a few people, made up his mind and then told everyone what to do. But that way the whole of

Jamesons would never fully share it. He had liked Leon's note. But progress was slow. I said: 'If you trust, I think they will fulfil that trust.'

A funny thing happened to our team. It was meant to be just 6 and me. But all kinds of people began wandering in and out. The young women on the switchboard came if they were not busy. Some secretaries and back room staff came. The office manager came. The directors came if they felt like it. Leon was clever and understood that good work can be done even if people are squashed on the floor and going in and out. Perhaps it reminded him of a rugby game! They insisted on having Sir Jeremy too. They invented more and more clever projects. But still nothing seemed to work. They could see nothing big enough to make a new business out of.

In one meeting a little thing came into my head. I hadn't said anything yet so I thought I'd better. I said:

'Excuse me. I think you do not understand what businesses do. Always you think they produce some kind of thing which people buy. It is a washing machine. It is a film. It is a nice meal. It is a computer. Even information is some kind of thing that people can buy. You are such materialisms!'

I shook with laughter and they looked at me a bit shocked. Sir Jeremy said: 'Do you mean materialists?' I said yes, probably.

Feeling brave, I went on: 'These are not what businesses really sell. They are not what their customers really buy.'

Leon said: 'Djalal what on earth are you talking about?'

I said: 'What businesses do is they produce things of the spirit that people like. They're qualities. Not things.'

Rob said: 'Like what?'

I said: 'Like love, of course. Beauty. Good fun. Friendship. These are what people really buy.'

There was a silence. Then Sir Jeremy said: 'My God!'

He went on: 'So what you are saying is that we have all been misunderstanding the nature of what we get up to all day.' I said: 'If you can understand this, then you will make a lot of money.'

The thin worried person had his head in his hands. He made a long wailing noise. It was as if I had changed his whole world. I had only said a very simple thing. I do not think the others understood yet.

Sir Jeremy said: 'I have spent years trying to rid myself of the materialist ways of thinking. With my head I have understood how scientists no longer see the universe as primarily a material system. When they look closely at the particles that make it up all they find is a mysterious empty space out of which matter and energy and so on appear and disappear. The whole thing to them is a value system, not a material one. But I've been brainwashed by the primitive material view of the world that I learned at school. It takes Djalal here to point the way back to what human beings have always known and always will know. We live in a value system, not a material one.'

The worried looking person said: 'I think everyone is realising this. It's only business that doesn't get it. Never mind that it's the same people. Business has got so much clutter around it. It can't change so easily.'

Leon was prowling excitedly round the room, occasionally kicking invisible rugby balls. Then he said:

'So we are presently in that case sitting on the threshold of one of the greatest marketing opportunities in the whole of history. It's like when hunters moved into farming; when farmers went into industry; when industry went into services and information. We're in transition now from things, services and information to qualities'.

Veronica said: 'And so what money is, it's the way we recognise the value, or quality that someone produces. We don't really buy a computer or a meal in a wonderful restaurant. We recognise the love and the intelligence that went into them and that they express.'

We all sat with a tight feeling in our stomachs. It comes

when there is much energy but not yet the knowledge of what to do with it. So it sits there, being uncomfortable. I slipped out quietly and went for a walk.

In our next meeting we made a list of qualities that might be the basis for our business of the future. As we did it we realised that many of them already were the basis of businesses. Only they probably did not realise it. Sometimes we laughed because we could not yet imagine how such qualities could ever make money. You will see later, though, that we were always wrong. I am sorry about the title which was Leon's idea:

DJALAL'S INVISIBLE NEW PRODUCTS

LOVE

BEAUTY

CARING

IMAGINATION

ENABLING

COMMUNITY

QUIETNESS

SPIRITUAL GROWTH

ADVENTURE

When You Come to Us Bring Music

DOING THINGS LOCALLY

TIME IN NATURE

TIME WITH ANIMALS

TIME WITH OTHER CULTURES

SLOWNESS

TOGETHERNESS

SIMPLICITY

CARING FOR THE LAND

EATING WELL

MUSIC AND DANCE

DIALOGUE

HEALING

SCIENCE AND DISCOVERY

TRUTHFULNESS

TEACHING

HAVING FUN

RELATING

COURAGE

INTELLIGENCE

SERVICE

As we made this list, which has kept growing, we knew it was somehow the basis for the products and the value of the future.

As for me, I was pleased there was not too much about the environment. Of course it is enormously important. But you do not all understand that it is only the humble start of a much bigger waking up of the spirit- a waking up to the needs of everyone and everything.

Now we had to work out how these wonderful new products could be part of our business. This was easy. Leon said:

'One of the things we know most about is raising the money to enable people to start businesses. Maybe that's what we want to do. But only businesses that want to do something useful and that understand Djalal's list of invisible products.'

Sir Jeremy was at that time sitting on the floor against a wall looking happy. He said: 'Yes. Maybe with one amendment. It might not always be money that they mainly need. If it's something else, we might try to provide that too.'

A fragment came to my mind from a poem that my master often quoted:

'When you come to us, bring music.'

Exactly! We would help others to sound their wonderful music in the world.

Chapter 6

A NEW KIND OF BUSINESS

At the end of the summer we all met again at Sir Jeremy's house. It was time to decide whether to take these ideas further into action, or leave them behind as an interesting diversion. If this was to happen, Jamesons would carry on as before and Sir Jeremy would find his own eccentric path elsewhere.

We soon worked on a statement of what our new objective for the company might be. This is what we came up with:

'Our aim is to finance, or actively support in any way we can, any business that we feel is useful'.

There was never really any doubt that we would go ahead. Over the weeks of discussion our ideas had gathered a kind of irresistible energy. But Leon made it easier for them to decide when he said:

'Since we began our discussions I have noticed two things that now seem obvious but I was blind to before.

First, out there in the ordinary world a spiritual revival of huge proportions is going on. Up to this point in history, real dedicated study and work aimed at individual growth and realisation was largely confined to a tiny minority within each of the religions. Now, it's commonplace. And it's commonplace not among cranks but among the young, the talented and the successful. I think I agree with those who say that this change in consciousness is reaching a sort of critical mass, like a nuclear reactor when the chain reaction starts. So it's gathering speed.

Secondly, I have been realising how Djalal's value driven businesses are in fact already all around us. They are most of the fastest growing and most exciting ones. One example is the huge growth of alternative health, whose basic product is not pills or surgery but love. It has grown spontaneously into a multi-million pound business sector, with no market research and minimal investment. Another is psychotherapy and various kinds of personal development, where the product is a change in consciousness. Another is the current revival in architecture which has moved from designing spirit-numbing tower blocks to expressing great beauty and revitalising communities. Another is the influx of high calibre people into businesses whose primary aim is to serve others – like running a cafe or looking after old people in their homes. These are signs of the new revolution in work. So I feel that as a company we do not have a choice. We have to get with it – or die, personally, spiritually and in due course economically.'

In the end, everyone agreed to the experiment. The next enormous step was to get our ideas accepted by the shareholders. When they heard of our plans, the majority were shocked, confused and then angry. Several threatened to sue on the grounds that profit is the only legal objective for a business. The meeting was almost a riot. But Sir Jeremy had a lot of the shares and had done some deals in advance (which he has never been very willing to talk about) with the others that mattered. So the vote was won, just.

Afterwards, I went with Sir Jeremy back to his home in the country, to celebrate with him and his wife.

At breakfast next morning the headlines in the newspapers were terrible. One was: 'Investment Company Loses Interest in Money'. Another said: 'Jamesons Decide to be Useful!' When Sir Jeremy got to the office, many journalists from TV and radio were waiting to talk to him. He explained quietly to each of them what he and his colleagues wanted to do and why. He didn't appear to care much what anyone thought. He just seemed to say: 'This is the dance we are doing. If you wish to join us you are welcome. If not, that is fine too.' In each interview, he invited anyone to contact Jamesons if they wanted to begin a business that was to be useful and to follow their spirit.

Sir Jeremy has told me that the next day was the biggest gamble of his life. The question was: would investors in Jamesons take all their money away? Or would they stay to see what happened?

Some investors did leave. But the pension funds and other city institutions, which had most of the money, had a problem. It began when one of the fund managers said on TV that he had already pulled out from this eccentric and irresponsible firm. The telephone began to ring from members of the public. They said: 'Have you got some of my money in Jamesons? Leave it there. That is exactly what I want to happen to some of it.' The companies which had got out began to sense a public relations disaster. In a few days they had to go back in. Some individuals with money invested directly in Jamesons removed a sensible portion of it. But a flood of others put in money, just for fun, to see what happened. Total funds increased. Jamesons gradually sold their holdings in businesses that they thought were not useful or actively harmful. They now had money in cash which even Sir Jeremy admitted was enormous. The great experiment had begun.

Neither Sir Jeremy nor anyone else had much idea what they were going to do with all this money. Was there anyone out there with good ideas? How would they find them? Would any of them have a business plan that showed the smallest chance of success?

They need not have worried. Within two months of all the talk in the newspapers and on TV, about two tons of business proposals had arrived, from all over the world. I asked my boss if we could store them in the car park. He agreed.

Now Sir Jeremy and Leon and the rest of the team had to work out what to do with all these proposals. Everyone in the whole company could not read them all.

They told me that companies usually solve this kind of problem by getting secretaries to throw away the proposals where the typing is not very good, or the English not very good, or the paper not very good. Then they are only interested in people who have a degree from a good university, who have most of the money already and have succeeded before so everyone can be sure they will do it again. Naturally, the investor has to make a lot of money as quickly as possible.

Leon and Sir Jeremy had different ideas. They went on TV and the radio again saying they were looking for talented people who had recently retired, or gone off to live a quieter life in the country. They needed to have special expertise in areas such as science, technology, business and the financial sector. They found many, many wonderful people like this. Usually, the reason they had left was that their spirit was unhappy.

Besides these people Leon and Sir Jeremy had been realising that there were other wonderful people of a different sort. These were ones who did not much like the business world of the 21st century. The environmental destruction and tremendous increase in inequality, especially, were not in tune with their spirit. Mostly, their journey had been inwards to find their own happiness and wisdom. Some of these people ran worthwhile but small businesses, like the ones that farm organically. Others worked for charities. Some had been for years in monasteries, or travelling. Some were therapists or healers of some kind. Often these people were unhappy, because they had not yet found big enough ways to express their spirit. So Leon and Sir Jeremy advertised for these people too.

Then, they made many little teams of these two sorts of people. They got on so well! It was like a love affair between those who had been apart for so long and now needed each other.

There were about 40 teams. Usually there were 4 in each. Each team came down to the parking bays and selected some proposals. Then it met with the proposers to refine and develop the ideas. We thought this would be impossible if the proposers were far away. But usually they managed. In the end there would be a smart proposal, in good English on the right paper.

Each finished proposal was considered by the full Jamesons team. To begin with, when deciding which projects to support, they often found themselves falling back into their old familiar ways of thinking which basically boiled down to the question: 'How much money will it make?' But then they would remember that their question now was: 'Will this project be useful? What invisible products will it manifest?'

Chapter 7

THE WORLD WE ACTUALLY WANT

At the time when they were ready to begin, it happened that just about everyone on the planet was wanting to be involved in the thrilling project of finding greener and more sustainable ways to do just about everything. Humanity was reinventing its core technologies and in so doing beginning to enjoy a totally revitalised global economy. Unless you have been living on Mars, you will be familiar with the thousands of wonderful new businesses that have arisen. Of course it was natural for many of them to come to Jamesons when they were starting or wanting to expand.

Jamesons took much bigger risks when they invested in new ways of producing food that did not involve pesticides, chemical fertilisers, habitat destruction, monocultures, weed killers, mechanical destruction of the soil and leaving the earth bare between crops so the planet got hotter and hotter. Jamesons massively backed the pioneers who were learning how to feed us sustainably. And already some swallows have reappeared where I live!

Sir Jeremy has told me that the fastest growing sector of his business was in what he calls 'artificial intelligence'. He gave me a disapproving look when I replied that it was nice to see big business showing intelligence of any kind. But apparently, so long as we control it, it can do a lot of useful things - like fraud prevention and inventing new medical drugs - better than us.

Some companies supported by Jamesons have been successful in areas where most of the opportunities seemed to have been used up already by well established companies. Trains, buses and airlines are examples. Most of them still operated according to an unconscious assumption that anyone who did not have their own transport must be a second class citizen, and should therefore be treated as such. So in the 21st century people still waited on freezing platforms, stood packed in carriages in conditions that would barely be legal for sheep, were herded in airport queues and jammed in minute seats with no leg room. Only very rich travellers could buy their way out of these miserable and degrading conditions. The new companies abandoned the class system and brought in the novel idea of trying to treat every traveller with dignity and respect throughout their journey. Of course, everyone wanted to book with them. Jamesons are now funding projects of this kind all over the world.

For a long time a few very large companies had got away with building houses that were ugly, inefficient, unsustainable, poorly built and very expensive. So Jameson businesses have done well building beautiful houses that heat themselves, make their own energy and dispose of their own waste. They are mostly made in factories instead of outside in the wind and rain and then simply delivered like any other product.

Something that may surprise you was that Jamesons supported many businesses that do very technical things for defence. Privileged people who have lived in safe areas do not always realise that humans can always be easily stirred into grasping more territory or committing atrocities in the name of some crazy belief system. Until that changes, we have to defend ourselves.

As the reputation of Jamesons grew its new businesses were increasingly all over the world. But I can only really tell you about some of the ones that have affected me in my little world.

I use an internet company - which I have to do to pay my electricity bill - begun by Jamesons that filters out all the horrible things that used to be on it. The original companies told us it was impossible to get rid of child abuse, violence, financial scams, fake news and false stories that destroyed the reputations and sometimes the lives of decent people. But it was only impossible because of the money they made. When kids drop in to see me, they use social media that are OK as well. It helps that no one is allowed to use them unless they give their correct name and address.

A change that made a big difference in the housing estate where I used to live is the health centre. If a person is ill most of the diagnosis is now done by computers. Since they gather information from all over the world they are mostly better at it than a doctor. Our doctors are now free to look after people's health instead of just giving out pills. They now run teams who help people to buy decent food, eat well, exercise, make friends, find useful work, have hobbies and fun, care for others in their community, sort out problems with housing and money and do all the other things that can make a person happy and stay well. It has been challenging for our doctors to change so deeply what they are doing and what they are for - but they are taking to it. There are no longer queues of people in their waiting rooms who have no hope of being well no matter what pills they are given or what operations are carried out.

An early challenge for doctors was when computers recommended treatments that they had been taught to regard as unscientific nonsense. There were quite a lot of these - Chinese herbs, Western herbs, acupuncture, alternative treatments for bad backs and hips, dance for treating depression, use of sound, meditation, yoga and even homeopathy. Computers did not worry about why treatments worked. They just collected information from around the world about what does work.

When Jamesons started, depression was dreadfully common among young people especially. Drugs companies made fortunes by selling pills and therapists got paid for talking with people. But neither made much difference. It took new thinking to admit that depression and other mental illnesses too are almost always caused by something being wrong in a person's life. So the new medical practices help identify what is wrong and then provide personal practical help to fix it. Older retired people with lots of life experience are great at helping with this. So at last we have treatment that actually works.

Another change that improved my life when I still lived on

the estate was computers watching the video cameras and starting action when they saw something bad. My life got safer. Life for single women who needed to get home at night got a million times safer. Some people objected to computers knowing so much, but they were privileged people who lived in safe places.

My local supermarket used to be full of junk food, sweets for the children, fizzy drinks and mostly pointless products wrapped in shiny plastic. I must admit I was pleased when a new Jameson business drove it into bankruptcy. The new supermarket sells fresh food at reasonable prices. There is no plastic. You bring your own containers for most things. The children are getting hooked on fruit and vegetables. Mothers do not have to resist the sweets and junk by the check outs. Most of the food is organic and produced by regenerative agriculture. Imaginative vegetarian food is on offer. The business organises trips for people to see and understand how their food is made. Nothing is described as 'healthy' or 'eco' when it isn't. Because of the cafe, it has become a community centre as well. There are notice boards that tell you about everything that is going on.

Jamesons is sometimes criticised for putting as much energy into small projects as into large ones. They reply that no one can tell which little projects will become enormous. A plan to preserve a few acres of forest in which people could re-establish sustainable ways of living has grown to cover thousands of square miles. An experimental environmentally sustainable village has led to the establishment of whole new cities that are thriving in previously empty areas – in deserts, remote areas of Eastern Europe and the highlands of Scotland. Something they all have in common is public spaces where people can meet - instead of being lonely in little private boxes.

Nowadays, governments often apply to Jamesons for funding for projects. They are usually projects that seem too idealistic for the taxpayers to pay for. A common scheme has been to help finance rewilding of huge areas and massive clean ups of wrecked environments, like rivers, coasts and inner cities. Somehow or other, even these make money.

Other projects arise from environmental organisations and pressure groups. Sometimes these apply to do things they have planned themselves, like to help homeless people build homes. Then there are no problems. But sometimes, because Rob and Sir Jeremy have a terrible sense of fun, they approach organisations who have been complaining about something for a long time. It is often cars, or chemical farming methods, or roads, or council estates, or the dirt in the sea. They ask the organisations what they would like to do. When they say what they would like, Jamesons says: 'Come on then, let's do it!' Then the people in the organisation find out that they never really wanted to do anything! What they wanted was to be on the outside of society and to complain about everything. So now they have to make a great journey, to be on the inside and take responsibility. It is very charming and rather funny. When this happens, Rob and Sir Jeremy often ask me to come along and spend some time with them.

Chapter 8

HOW IT WORKS

I had better tell you a bit more about how the business works.

When businesses are financed by Jameson & Co it is different from how it used to be. I have seen the computers which used to tell them when to sell a share that was going down. The computer did not say how many people might have to be made redundant, or how much suffering was caused. Jamesons new investors become more like partners in businesses. If a business has problems, they are everyone's problems, not a signal to pull out. The expertise among investors is often mobilised to help companies out of difficulties. Even in normal times regular meetings take place attended by investors, employees, customers and anyone from the community who wants to come along. These are creative meetings, to dream of new products and markets and ways of doing things. Managers look forward to these events. After each, they find their ideas have moved on; new possibilities have appeared.

Jameson businesses that wanted to be public were reluctant to use the existing stock exchanges, which had become more like casinos and refuges for every kind of financial crook. So they began their own stock exchange which simply provides long term investment and support for real businesses.

Some things have not changed. Jamesons is still tough. Any business it has money in has to report as rigorously as ever. It also has to be much more open than was normal before. When a business is failing Jamesons is as prepared as ever to cut the losses and close it down. The difference is that the failure is seen as a team failure. Somehow they have not read their own or their customers' spirit right. The Jameson contact network is then mobilised to try to find work for those who have lost their jobs, perhaps to continue their work in a different way.

The success of most of the companies begun by Jamesons has helped get rid of that myth about competitiveness. Of course it sometimes helps them to be better, or cheaper or faster than another company. But we can all see that what really makes businesses succeed is when they are useful and work with spirit and with love. Then the producer's energy flows, the organisation works and the customers respond.

Jamesons are especially keen to get rid of the idea of competitiveness when they work internationally. Veronica once said to me that competing with a culturally rich but technologically simple people is like a dinosaur having a fight with a delicate flower. Of course the dinosaur wins every time. In reality though it loses. Imagine how much beauty it could have experienced! Think of the perfume it could have enjoyed! So Jamesons do not compete. They cooperate, in love.

Jamesons does not give much to charity. The company has accepted that its own particular interest is in creatively avoiding the need for charity, by generating jobs, community, things to do, healthy places to live and so on. It is a basically creative rather than a basically caring organisation. Our focus is all the time on helping people to take power themselves to fulfil their own dreams; we are reluctant to gather power to care for others.

The Jameson office in London has become a great source of fun for the press. Sir Jeremy said that he wanted to bridge the gap between home and work, personal life and business life. So the offices have become full of pictures, plants, squash rackets, rugs, books and even pets. People have paid for their windows to be got to open. What the press like most is the foyer. Employees had wanted to start a crèche so their children could be looked after. Since there was no spare room, the only possible space was the ridiculously grand entrance hall. Now it is full of children. There have been cartoons of ministers applying for loans to 6 month olds. Most people play with the children for a while before they come in.

A very important part of the office now is the restaurant. We all take the food and cooking most seriously. The cooks are celebrities. The quality of what they provide affects the energy of the whole business. Lunch is where the most creative business happens. There are no social divisions and people are encouraged to sit with people they don't normally spend time with. Often I see young secretaries arguing with directors. I see cyclists who run errands for the business trying to sell projects to analysts. I see visitors from a rain forest being asked how *their* business works. I see green activists finding out that some of the corporate types have done more for the environment than they could even imagine. Often I see government ministers come to find out what is going on. On one wall a huge board lists current projects and there are photographs all over the others. In old companies all these things were secret but Jamesons are usually very pleased if someone else finds out and wants to get involved.

On warm days lunch spills into the street. Jamesons has managed to get it pedestrianised. After lunch new ideas and dreams for projects fly around the computer networks. In the evening the restaurant is more of a club, open to all. Someone comes to play or sing.

By the way, Sir Jeremy wanted to invent some kind of job for me. He said it did not matter what I did and I did not really have to do anything. He just wanted to have me about. Well, I was already entitled to my pension and did not need a job. So I decided to come in and make tea and coffee for everyone on three mornings each week. It was nice to see them all and we had little chats. I was everyone's grandfather I think.

There is quite a high turnover of staff at Jamesons. Some need a rest from the speed of it all. Also, investment analysts, brokers and others (you see, I even know some of their names now) sometimes get so involved in a business they have helped create that they naturally drift over into it. Often the government asks to borrow people. It seems that every clever graduate wants to come to us and there is always a queue of qualified people hoping to join.

Many of those alternative people who began in Rob and Sir Jeremy's teams have come into the business. They have had great influence in helping to change the culture from money to one of spirit and usefulness. Sir Jeremy jokes that he is no longer sure whether he is running a company or a spiritual community that makes money. Many now, like him, struggle to express in their work much more than a personal, limited and frightened individual self, primarily concerned only with its own survival. Their wish is to express a greater self that is more universal in its outlook.

Chapter 9

CHANGES WE NEVER IMAGINED

After Jamesons had been going successfully for a few years, I think even Sir Jeremy thought that they had done more or less all they could. Besides helping to start useful businesses around the world they had helped to bring the basic underlying ideas about capitalism more into line with the cares and needs of real people.

It was one day at lunch however that a chain of events began that in due course made us realise that we had only just begun.

I was in the restaurant with 15 years old Ayesha, who was getting some work experience. She was an employee's daughter I think. As we were chatting a tall woman who gave an immediate impression of being powerful came up and said to me:

'Am I right in thinking that you are Djalal? I'm told that you have some influence round here'.

'Well' I replied, 'I used to be the car park attendant'.

Her eyes twinkled. But then they told me that our meeting was about to be serious. She said:

'I'm Arabella. I'm in public relations'.

Ayesha said:

'What's that?'

Her answer was not quite what I expected:

'We tell stories to the public that enable very rich organisations to get even richer'.

'Like what?' Ayesha asked.

'Well, we tell you that you can't change to electric cars because of range anxiety. We tell you that pesticides and chemical fertiliser are the only way to feed people. We tell you that you can't possibly build a house in the countryside. We tell you that smoking is a question of individual freedom. We tell you that poor people need to have processed food because it's cheaper than fresh food. We tell you that social media companies cannot possibly change their algorithms.'

Ayesha interrupted: 'That's a load of shit'.

I thought that Arabella might ask for this insolent teenager to be thrown out, but instead noticed a flash of mutual recognition pass between them. She seemed to need to continue:

'We tell you that it is completely impossible to tax very rich international companies. We tell you that hedge funds and speculators perform a useful function in correcting markets. We tell you that the only way to cure depression is to take the pills. We tell you that your health service is the best in the world even though we know it is mind blowingly inefficient. We tell you that our clients are doing their very best to prevent sewage going into the sea and chemicals poisoning our rivers. We tell you that food can only be safely delivered wrapped in plastic'.

Finally she said: 'Our latest creation is environmental, social and governance ....'

Luckily, before Ayesha could deliver another insult on behalf of all the world's despairing and disbelieving teenagers, Sir Jeremy appeared. When Arabella introduced herself he said:

'I know who you are. You are head of PR at our biggest oil company. Before that it was agro-chemicals wasn't it? And you're the distinguished head of your trade organisation'.

Not being one for beating around the bushes, he simply said:

'Are you here to join us?'

That was how Arabella came to take us into what she calls grown up territory that we had not expected.

The first thing she did was set up a communications business that gently but persistently demolished what Veronica calls the dinosaur stories. We didn't know how to finance the huge budgets that would be needed but to Aarabella it was obvious. Lots of the super rich were thrilled to be associated with the idea of promoting spiritually orientated business. Once they had made enough money, this was often quite genuinely the direction they wanted to go in themselves.

When Veronica got involved, she pointed out that it is seldom a good idea to engage dinosaurs in combat. They are, after all, enormously powerful and in the case of business have immense expertise. The thing with a dinosaur is to gradually and lovingly seduce it. The consequence of this approach was that numbers of them began to do good things. And now the whole business world has changed so fundamentally that there is no going back.

But Arabella wasn't finished yet. It was part of her normal job to be in regular touch with politicians. After all, she said, it is their job to create conditions in which businesses can thrive and wonderful things get done. But many, including the very best, were giving up and leaving. They were fed up with the incredible rudeness of interviewers. They were fed up with constant state funded ridicule on radio and TV dressed up as comedy. Even worse than that, they felt that the media were interested in their own agenda and were no longer willing to pay attention to the very genuine concerns and ideas of those highly intelligent and knowledgeable people known as the British public. And when politicians did manage to put in place a good policy, the civil service would mess it up.

Arabella might have given up, but instead she founded a new news channel. This had totally different rules. Politeness. Listening. Openness to new ideas. No covert promotion of media companies' group think. Reporting the good and exciting as well as the bad. Compassion. No lazy categorizations such as 'Left', 'Right' or 'progressive' (which means it fits the agenda of the broadcaster). Ideas and projects are simply good or not so good wherever they come from. At last the public are getting a chance to hear fresh ideas from the many brilliant people around the world.

This new channel is helping to bring the most talented people back into politics. People are voting for them because at last they are hearing the real issues of our time discussed and seriously addressed. Already we can see enormously important new businesses arising as a result of what they are doing.

Here is one example. Until recently, it was commonly accepted that it was too difficult to build enough houses for everyone. So many were homeless and few of the young could ever hope to own a property. But it emerged that the lack of housing was the result of deliberate policy. No one (except the very rich) was allowed to build a house in the countryside. When the law got changed, people have built in vast areas of the UK that were not much good for anything else. Many of the houses are beautiful, original and sustainable. People can build a mansion or a tiny home according to what they want and can afford. The countryside is coming back to life and creative new economies are developing.

The new politicians have also brought about huge improvements in health. The British public had been convinced that only their National Health Service could deliver health. The media treated it with unchallenged respect. But the reality gradually emerged that, even though there were many wonderful employees, the organisation was out of date, inefficient, in some cases corrupt and sometimes even descending into neglect and cruelty. So Jamesons have been allowed to fund new organisations to deliver health care. Their purpose, of course, is not to make money but to deliver good care.

Something similar has happened with the civil service. One reason why the national mood had become so despairing was that when politicians announced sensible projects nothing would happen. Or else the project would get so messed up that it would be abandoned. So Jamesons have funded organisations that compete for the work the civil service was supposed to be doing. Because they only needed about half the staff they could pay people well and so attract the best.

Perhaps the most thrilling changes of all have been for wildlife. The new politicians have not accepted the idea that taxpayers should pay for farmers in the highlands of Wales and Scotland to produce not very much and at the same time exterminate wildlife. So thousands of square miles are now being rewilded. And these areas are now more valuable and employ more people than before.

The most recent development is that even parts of the sea are being protected and totally destructive fishing techniques are stopped.

Some issues, like immigration and the role of incoming religions remain unsolved. But at least we now have realistic discussion about them which is a start. The public can now dare to express their real opinions without the threat of being politically incorrect or even sent to prison.

My latest impression is that the Jameson funded media company is now giving a lot of time to the many brilliant people around the world who are thinking about entirely new economic systems. That may sound surprising but it is, after all, only a few hundred years since we invented the present one.

Chapter 10

THE MARRIAGE OF SPIRIT AND BUSINESS

Three years ago, when I was 76, I decided to spend my last years in the countryside. I now live in a tiny hut in the middle of the Jamesons' farm, about two miles from a road. It is in a beautiful spot, in an old wood beside a lake that Sir Jeremy made many years ago. Here, I thought, I could be quiet and indulge my love of birds, animals and nature. But I have not been quite as quiet as I expected!

Every week or so, I see a figure or two coming walking down the path to my cottage, and I know it is probably someone from Jamesons.

Sometimes, they are full of worries about a deal they are doing. Nearly all of them have in the past been on courses to find out how to give the other person as little as possible. When they manage this, they are supposed to come home very happy in the evening! But in fact they are miserable. Now they want to give as much as they can. But how much can they afford? This is difficult. So we talk things through. Often, you know, they are better at loving the others than at loving themselves, so I remind them of that.

Another difficulty they have, as they grow in spirit, is to be realistic. When people – like most of those in the old businesses – are still very small and frightened, they are naturally suspicious of others; they see them as bad, stupid or out to harm or cheat them. As night follows day, the others often respond in just the way that is expected! But as people grow, they see the beauty in others. Of course the others are touched and usually give honour and kindness in return. But not always! I try to help the young idealists in Jamesons to realise that the beauty in others includes all their imperfections. When they see this, they can be realistic.

They get in a muddle, too, about the balance between creativity and destruction. Sometimes they think that creating can always be done softly and gently; it is a kind of feebleness that can come in the early stages. I explain to them that often, in order to create, it is necessary first to leave behind what was there before. I remember a bishop who came to see me about an issue of this kind. He was naturally fond of the magnificent old churches in his diocese. But they were freezing and impossibly expensive to look after. So he wanted to pull some of them down, sell the land and use the money to build modern centres suitable for real study and practice. He dreamed that they would be used by people from all traditions, so this might mean replacing many of the clergy. I asked him if he knew in his spirit that this was his desire. He said he did. And now his problem is how to look after so many people who come!

Those who are growing often go through a period of finding disagreement difficult; they get the idea that spirituality is all about giving one another hugs! But this is only one aspect of love. A greater aspect is to be able to say fearlessly what is true for each one of us in each moment. The trick is to do so in love and unattached to who is right or wrong. Honest disagreement, when it occurs in this way, can lead to solutions that no one could have imagined at the beginning.

A few weeks ago Leon came to see me because he was worried that meetings at Jamesons were becoming less 'business-like' as he called it. When I asked him what he meant he said a lot of time was being taken up by people's personal feelings. In meetings people were increasingly being openly tired, ill, happy, depressed, tearful, jealous, insecure, confused, angry or enthusiastic just like real people! As we talked, he seemed to assume that decisions could be taken either quickly with the logical, thinking mind, or inefficiently on the basis of emotions. As he talked more, he recognised that those emotions and feelings often hold very important information for their projects. Leon, you see, is just now learning to think/feel, instead of doing one and then the other.

I urge them all to watch and learn from Sir Jeremy in these areas. Another thing he demonstrates is how it is not always a gift to others to be nice to them. His favourite target, when he is on TV, is management consultants. He tells them they all pay attention to *how* to run a business. But what matters is *what* a business is doing. They know in their spirit that he is right, but he undermines their narrowness and limitation of vision. So they get very upset.

I always have time to see Veronica, who has become a great friend. Recently she was feeling challenged when investors asked how they could measure the success of a Jameson company. It used to be so simple: money.

'How can I', she asked, 'measure the output of your invisible products?'

After some thought I proposed: 'Well, the existing units of

measurement are inches, centimetres, kilos, litres, fluid ounces, temperature, embodied energy …. I can't think of any others'.

'I suppose embodied energy might work for love anyway'.

Attempting to be serious, I said:

'I suggest they ask any young person. They know how to just pay attention and *know*. Best of all ask Ayesha; she'll give it to them straight'.

We laughed. Ayesha works for Arabella now. She is one of those rare people who is fearless. All that matters is truth. Arabella says she has so much energy she worries that she might one day cause an explosion.

Recently, Veronica has been leading Jamesons into a new activity for the company. It began by accident when, coincidentally in the same week, a head teacher and a manager of a hospital asked her to visit. I remember her fury when she came to see me! She said: 'Djalal, both of these good people I met were on the edge of a breakdown. I could soon see why. Government holds them strictly accountable for their work. But it doesn't give them the freedom to do it. I passed corridors of pointless managers filling in pointless forms. As far as I could tell, most of the staff had either given up or took as many months off work each year with stress related illnesses as they could get away with. I don't blame them.

I'd go nuts, or actively homicidal, in a couple of weeks.'

'What would be the solution?' I asked.

'Mark all incoming government e mails as junk.'

'So what's the solution?' I asked again, and saw her at last relax and begin to imagine.

'Well, I think just about everyone now realises that organisations are like people; they get conceived, grow up with enthusiasm, mature and in due course wither and die. Most of ours have got advanced degenerative disease, if not actual rigor mortis. So why don't we give others a chance to have a go? Then teachers could teach, doctors could heal, benefits could reach those that actually need them .... and so on.'

It was this conversation, together with Arabella's revolution in communications, that led to Jamesons becoming involved in finding new ways to deliver essential services all over the world. The methods seldom included privatisation, because it tended to replace incompetence with highly competent pursuit of profit. Instead, Jamesons have become involved in developing new structures designed to enable groups of skilled people to be of service if they wish to. As ever with Jamesons, while profit may be a necessary strategy in some cases, it is never an objective.

When Veronica came last week she said: 'Dalal, this is

crazy. We are supposed to be a business. And now we are up to our neck in projects which are about society and community. I doubt we'll ever make any money out of it.' I said to her:

'Veronica, what do you think a business is?'

She said rather huffily: 'It's an organisation that follows its spirit and makes money, of course.' I went and made some tea to give her time to think. When I came back she said:

'Alternatively, I suppose you could say a business is a bunch of people who are busy together.' I smiled, feeling very pleased. She said:

'Djalal, you are the most outrageous revolutionary I have ever come across.' But I had not said anything at all! Veronica was just a little shocked by her own daring in seeing something so simple.

More recently, Veronica, Sir Jeremy and I have continued the conversation. How can a business move beyond money, to do whatever its spirit moves it to do? Of course we do not yet know the answers, but we have decided it is good and to continue our work with communities.

The company is still fairly small. We are no more than about 300. We still rely a lot on a huge pool of talent among the retired and others who do not need to earn much.

I expect you are wondering then how it can be that Jamesons is now known to almost everyone. This year we have been voted the most valuable business name in the world. We are the fastest growing business and the one that most people would like to work for. I will tell you. It is all rather odd.

What has happened is that every business we have helped to create has been proud of their connection with Jamesons. Some of them began to call themselves 'A Jameson Company'. The others followed – even if sometimes we had not done much at all. The name began to show up all over the world. Always it was associated with projects that were in some way useful and in tune with people's real dreams. Often it is used by companies that we no longer have anything to do with and may not even know exist. It has no status in law. The lawyers worry a great deal about what to do and say we are losing colossal sums of money. The name should at least be franchised. Sir Jeremy just thinks it is terribly funny. Jamesons has become a symbol for a new kind of business, with a different intention. So we give up and enjoy it instead.

Every now and then Jameson people ask if they can begin a similar venture of their own, often in some distant part of the world. Sir Jeremy always encourages them. They too become 'A Jameson Company', whatever that is. And so it goes on. He cheerfully advises competitors how to do it too.

Chapter 11

CONCLUSION

Nowadays I am getting slower and I am allowing my spirit to become finer as my death approaches. Every day Sir Jeremy's old gamekeeper comes to feed the otters that he breeds on the lake to help repopulate the rivers. He calls for a chat and to make sure I am alright.

When people come I think it is helpful for them to see that it is possible to be happy with few possessions and only plants, birds and animals as my principal friends. Shopping, you know, is a hopeless path to happiness!

When people from the company visit, I remind them not to get caught up in all their good actions and projects. The foundation for the business is always the inner work that they do because, you see, the outer work always expresses what is inside. So if there is anger, greed, violence, desire for control or power, or a wish to achieve just to satisfy the ego, these will emerge in every project no matter how well intentioned it may be. If there is love, and the desire to serve and be of use, these will likewise be present in what is created.

My greatest pleasure is when Sir Jeremy walks over in the evenings and we go down to the lake together. He is away a lot, talking and lecturing around the world, but sometimes he is here. We watch the otters and listen to the blackbirds and then the moorhens going to bed. Centuries ago this was something everyone could enjoy. Now at last we are finding our way back to this place – but in a different and more conscious way.

A few weeks ago, he told me something of great importance. He had been away on a retreat. Sir Jeremy said that, after the first few days, he had been able to sit in a state of very intense and clear awareness, beyond thought, feelings, emotion and sensation. He had found his way at last to the kind of consciousness that he fell into by accident all those years ago in the car park. This time, it had come easily as a result of his years of study and meditation. He said:

'Now I realise something that I had never before comprehended so fully. It is that I, and the rest of the universe, are basically, intrinsically alright as we are. I do not therefore have to do anything in order to validate myself. I am valid anyway.'

I knew what his answer would be, but I asked him all the same: 'Are you therefore going to do nothing from now on?'

He said: 'On the contrary. I am freer to do whatever seems appropriate, to be for good. This is my motivation.'

I said: 'It is only when more people reach this realisation that we might be able to save our planet and our own species. Because then we can stop this manic race for achievement, which is mostly a race to destroy.'

He said: 'I'm not optimistic that this will happen in time. Maybe it doesn't matter so much as we think. Something else will evolve. They may be wiser than us.'

A few evenings ago, in our favourite spot by the water as usual, we carried our thoughts further.

Sir Jeremy said: 'If things are alright as they are, why are some actions better than others?'

I said: 'The only answer I have is that the universe contains within it a desire to express love. That is what the whole thing is a manifestation of. So we act well when we play our part in this.'

Sir Jeremy said: 'That fits with an experience that has been growing in me. I feel that in every moment I take in energy from the universe, and with each action I give it out again in my own way. In this way the universe itself somehow develops and grows.'

'Yes. And what so many had lost sight of when you came back to the company from South America, was that the most important opportunity we all have to express this love in the universe is through our work. This is how we grow, and it grows.'

'And all this love, does it have a point or do we just take it as a given?'

'Well', I replied, 'at home in Turkey we say the purpose of love is for God to know himself. God is lover, love and beloved.'

We listened for a while as the last birds found a place to roost and everything fell silent around the lake. Then Sir Jeremy asked: 'Djalal, do you think it matters what each of us does? Has each of us some special purpose?'

I said: 'Actually I think there are great dangers in this view. It can be a big ego trip. Or a person can waste a lifetime trying to find out.'

'So how do people know what to do?'

I said: 'Anything useful.'

Sir Jeremy asked: 'And what if they can't find a useful job?'

I said: 'There are always useful jobs, even if they are humble. But if not, then they must beg or starve. Anything is better than doing something destructive.'

Sir Jeremy looked at me, laughing, and said: 'Djalal, you're holding something back.'

I said: 'Yes. It is because we should be careful about saying this to people too soon, before they are ready. When people have really worked, spiritually and psychologically, to clear away the debris that covers up their real spirit, they find that certain activities, and the expression of certain qualities, really resonate for them. The atoms in the body literally vibrate with life. This is when they discover what they are here to do. That of course is why you re-started Jamesons, and are now guiding it in its new direction. It is why I worked quietly in a car park for years. I didn't know why, but it felt right.'

Sir Jeremy said: 'And this as I understand it is the true meaning of the resurrection story. To find out who we are, the familiar self has, literally, to die. We may have to abandon all its dreams for a nice comfortable life. It's no less painful each time it happens. But each time it does, we wake up a bit more to who we really are.'

Before I end, I would like to tell you why I have written this story. It is not because we at Jamesons have discovered some new answer to business that I would like to convince you about. What we have done works fairly well now, but I expect we will need different answers in a few years time.

No. I have written it because I want to invite you to dream. I want to help you to break out a little more from the prison of old ideas and beliefs that we all hedge ourselves in with. I want to show you that, if we can manage to dream, fulfilling the dream is really quite easy. It may not happen in the way you expect but nevertheless something does happen!

And this of course is according to the nature of spirit. It gives us no certainties. Nothing is definitely true or not true, right or wrong. As soon as anyone ties it down, it is no longer there. Spirit is like a wave. If we pay attention to it, and can stand being in such a place of freedom, we can balance right in the hissing, foaming crest of the wave. Of course we fall off every now and then. But on the whole we can be there, which is a good thing because this is where we are happy.

I suppose another thing that Sir Jeremy and his colleagues at Jamesons have shown is that to do good things we do not have to wait for anyone else. Governments and all those other institutions far away are mostly thrilled with what we do. The only people we really have to wait for are ourselves. I wish it had not taken so long for everyone to realise that.

I believe the wave of spirit is moving faster and faster. Therefore I expect that over the next few years you will see many rules of work and business that you are familiar with changing and falling down, like a pack of cards. Please do not be afraid. It happens every now and then. It may even be that most of the existing economy will collapse. It does not matter; something new will come in its place.

Now that I have finished this story I think I will die soon. I am old and fragile and have done about as much as I can. I have meditated often on death and, as many have said before me, it is only through doing this that I have been able to enjoy my life fully.

As for Sir Jeremy, he says he wants to do less. But there are so many demands on him that he finds it difficult and I worry for his health. I have said to him that if he will only sit quietly just as much will happen in the world, but he is not quite ready to hear that yet!

Looking back at when these events began, of course some people were doing marvellous things. But on the whole capitalism as it was then understood was taking us close to the gates of hell. It was on the way to destroying us, the living world and the planet. So we changed the rules and now it is giving us hope.

If you are reading this and have a business, or are thinking of starting one, I send you my love. You can play a part in reinventing every single business and industry, so as to meet the dreams and aspirations of people today.

And Good Luck!

Acknowledgements

A lot of people have taught me stuff. But I would most especially like to thank Pir Vilayat Inayat Khan for his inspiration. I think this book is pretty much a rewrite of what he used to teach.

About the Author

I spent 20 years working in documentary films - as editor, cameraman, writer and then director. After a horrific year in globally influential public relations, I trained and then worked as a transpersonal psychotherapist. A degree in law from Cambridge University was occasionally useful. Many years studying Indian psychology and spiritual practice were more useful.

I live with my wife Pat on a south facing hillside in North Wales where we grow our own vegetables and (with help from Elon Musk) generate a lot of our own energy. I am currently restoring 5 acres of ancient oak wood and four acres of meadow for the benefit of wildlife. At the age of 78 I still play tennis for North Wales which is completely ridiculous.

I have two sons and a step daughter, all very successful (and useful).

PS. It is really great to hear from people. My e-mail address is michael@sclater.co.uk.

Printed in Poland
by Amazon Fulfillment
Poland Sp. z o.o., Wrocław

31068264R00060